Out to Lunch

Peggy Perry Anderson

Houghton Mifflin Company
Boston 1998

To Jack, Jorie, Jeffery and Jinger,
our nieces and nephews
who prepared us for parenthood.

Library of Congress Cataloging-in-Publication Data

Anderson, Peggy Perry.
   Out to lunch / by Peggy Anderson.
      p.   cm.
   Summary: A mischievous frog makes a scene when his parents take
him to a fancy restaurant to eat.
   ISBN 0-395-89826-9
   [1. Restaurants—Fiction.   2. Behavior—Fiction.   3. Frogs—
Fiction.   4. Stories in rhyme.]   I. Title.
PZ8.3.A54840u   1998
[E]—dc21   97-30836
                                                                           CIP
                                                                            AC

Walter Lorraine Books

Copyright © 1998 by Peggy Perry Anderson

WOZ   10   9   8   7   6   5   4   3   2   1

"Out to eat.
What a treat!"

"Too bad," Joe's mother said,
"our babysitter was sick in bed."

"We're ready to eat.
Just give us a seat!"

"Do you have crayons or playgrounds?"
asked Joe.

The waiter said no.

"Mind your manners well today.
We're out to lunch, not out to play."

"I'll have pie and cake.
NO PEAS!"

Mother said,
"One child's meal, please."

"I'm a reindeer!" said Joe.

"Now where did he go?"

"Peek-a-boo! I see you."

"Remember what I said today.
We're out to lunch, not out to play."

"Yippee! Yippee! Food for me!"

Joe slurped.

Joe burped.
"Uh-oh,"
said Joe.

BRRRRRUP!

"There's an itch on my toe."

"The table is no place for feet.
Please, Joe, sit still and eat."

Joe dropped his fork.

Joe dropped
his spoon.

Joe launched his
fish stick to the moon.

"JOE, SIT STILL!"

"Oh, dear.
There's a fly in here!"

"Don't worry. I'll get him, Dad!"

WHAP!

ZAP!

"Best fly I ever had!"

"Okay, Joe, it's time to go."

"Out to eat. What a treat!"